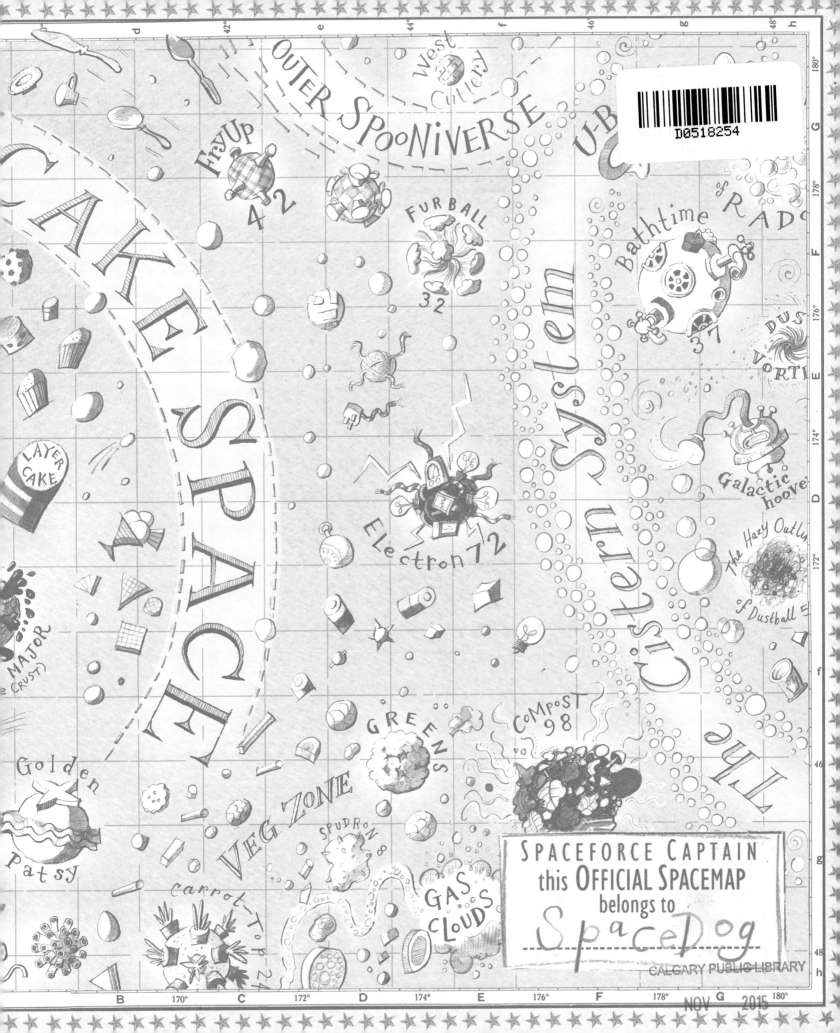

SPACE DOG

Mini Grey

Alfred A. Knopf
New York

It's the year **3043** and, for as long as anyone can remember, on **HOME PLANET**

ASTRO

SPACE DOGS,

have been **SWORN**

R FELINEKIND

ASTROFORCE
NEWS
YOUR DAILY DIGEST

ASTROCATS
LAND ON
SATURN

D THE MILKY WAY
Destination
Dairy Quadrant
renamed
'Caturn'

amery Major

Remember:
DON'T TALK

TO
SPACEDOG

THE DAILY RODENT
NEW CHEESE DISCOVERIES
CHEESE ON THE CARDS
IN SPACE

LATEST SPACE NEWS
IN THE DAILY RODENT

TRAINING

If it's there, the
moustronauts will find it.
*Crack collecting team are
off in their cheesular modules.*

Latest mission: to the Dairy Quadrant
to retrieve Cheese Samples
from the legendary mines of Cheesoid 5

A CHEESE ANT
of CHEESOID 5 -
believed harmless

CHEESOID 5

AT THE MOUSEFORCE BASE

MICE ON THE MOON

BEWARE
THE ASTROCAT

The cheese ants
mostly harm

First stop on the quest will be
sampling the surface of Stiltron 9 –
where the atmosphere is feared to
be disturbingly pungent. Our mice
will have to tak

This mor   the first   of
brave

ENEMIES.

*(After all, that's the
way it has always been.)*

But there's no time
for that now,
because . . .

. . . in the vast deeps of space
a small ship is zooming.

At last,
Space Dog
is about
to go

HOME.

It has been a long mission
sorting out planetary problems
in the Dairy Quadrant.

It all started with distress calls
from the Breakfast Cluster.

Space Dog—we need help!
Our planet is suffering
from a terrible dryness!
All our milk lakes have dried up.
We can't carry on like this.

Space Dog—we're awash with
milk! Our homes are flooding—
we haven't got much time.

Sure enough, the atmosphere
on Cornflake 5 was much
too dry and crunchy . . .

. . . whereas nearby Bottleopolis
was afloat with milk.

So dry!
So dry!

Thundering
milkswamps!
I'd better hurry. . . .

Aaargh, so
very dry!

Glug glug!

Splutter!

It looked like a job
for Space Dog.

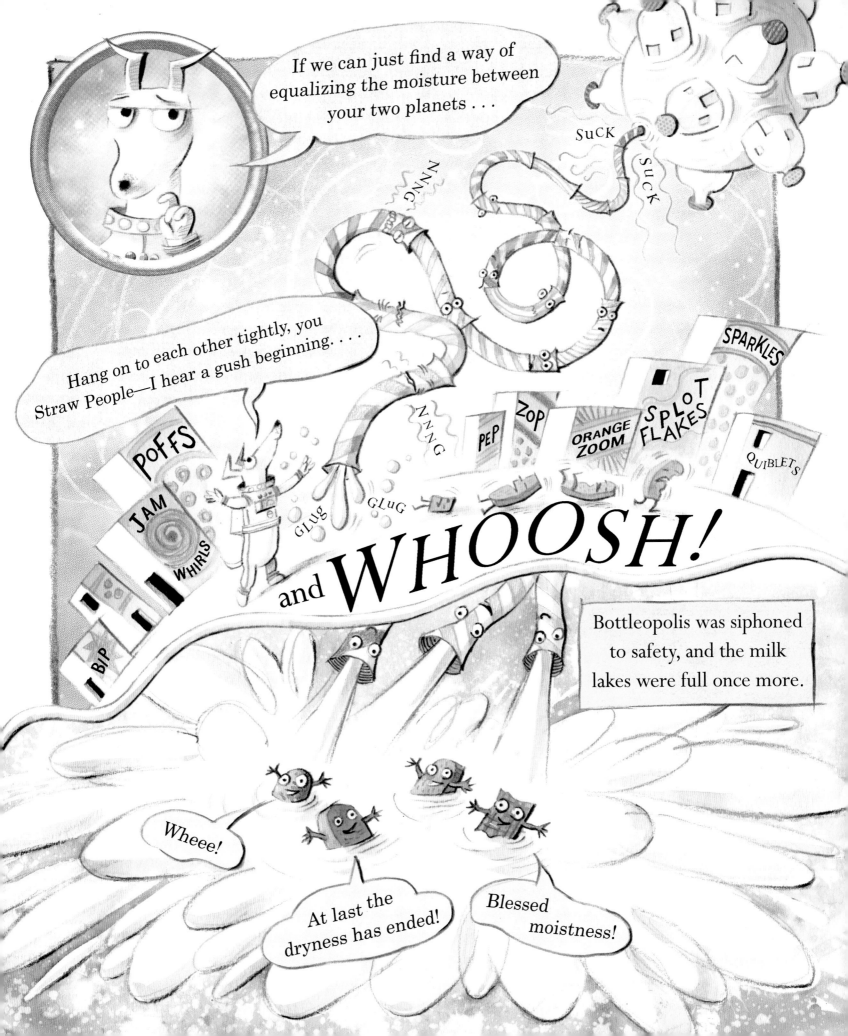

Things carried on . . .

with the evacuation of a Colossal Stink from Bath Time 37,

making contact with a Spaghetti Entity in the Pastaroid Belt, and rescuing the people of Niblet 12 from an escaped pet that had gone on the rampage.

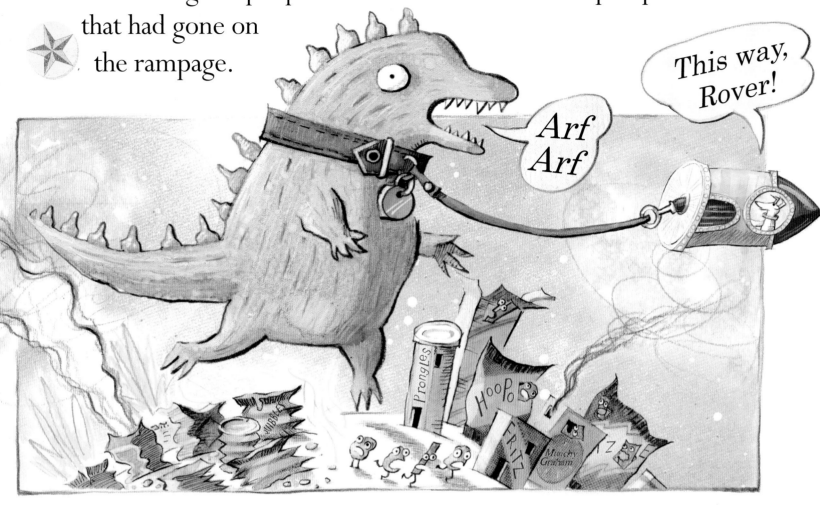

Then there was just time to judge a hat competition . . .

. . . before Space Dog returned to his ship, the SS *Kennel*.

Time to go home.

At least there are plenty of supplies
in Space Dog's cupboard.

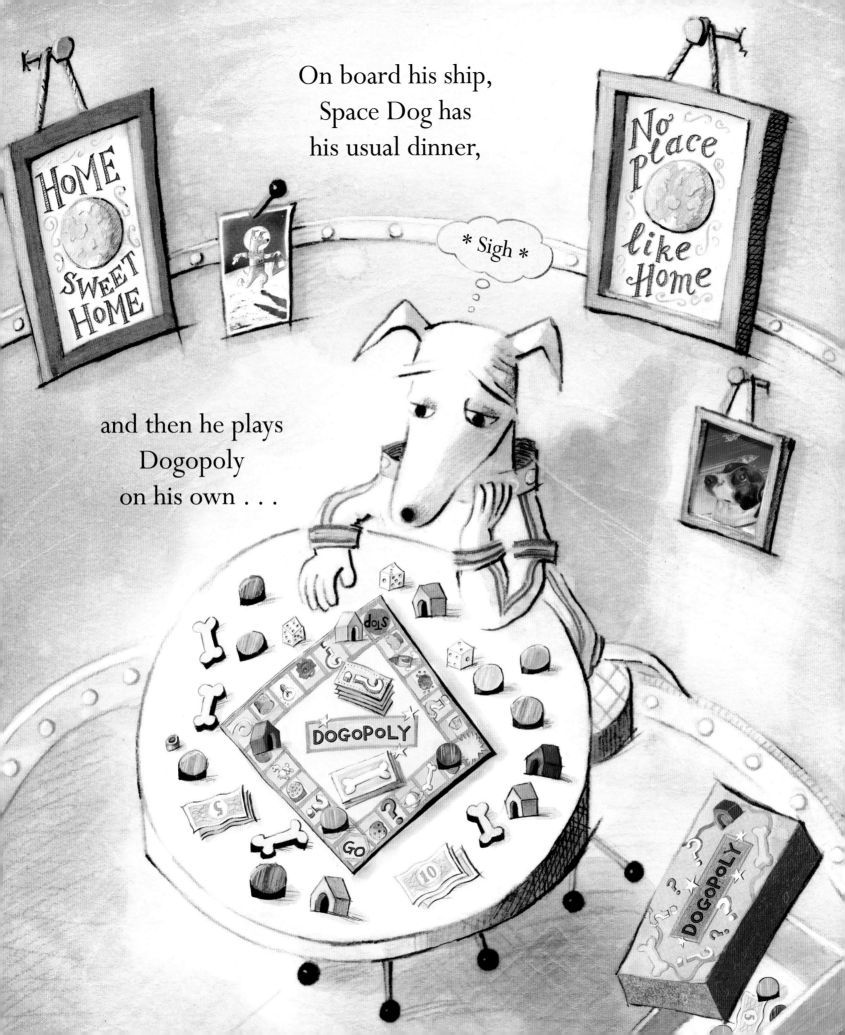

On board his ship,
Space Dog has
his usual dinner,

and then he plays
Dogopoly
on his own . . .

. . . before he sleeps in his bunk
and dreams of his Home Planet,
shining like a beautiful marble
in space.

HOME PLANET

Meanwhile

somewhere not so far away in the Dairy Quadrant, Astrocat is also zooming in his saucer.

Mmmm. Destination: Cream!

Suddenly Space Dog is woken by a distress call
coming through on his Laser Display Screen.

The saucer is sinking too quickly to be rescued,
but Space Dog pulls out the occupant.

AN ASTROCAT!

"But Astrocats and Space Dogs are Sworn Enemies!" gulps Astrocat.

"But there's no time for that now!" says Space Dog.

Space Dog drags Astrocat out of the thick cream and takes him aboard his own ship.

Your saucer is lost— you'd better hitch a ride on the SS *Kennel*.

GLUG

DANGER

What in CakeSpace am I going to do with an **Astrocat** on board?

When Astrocat has dried off . . .

I think you'll find, Space Dog, that your bone has landed on my kennel.

Well, I'll be jiggered! Not a bad move there, Astrocat. I'll have to up my game, playing you!

. . . it turns out he is surprisingly good at playing Dogopoly,

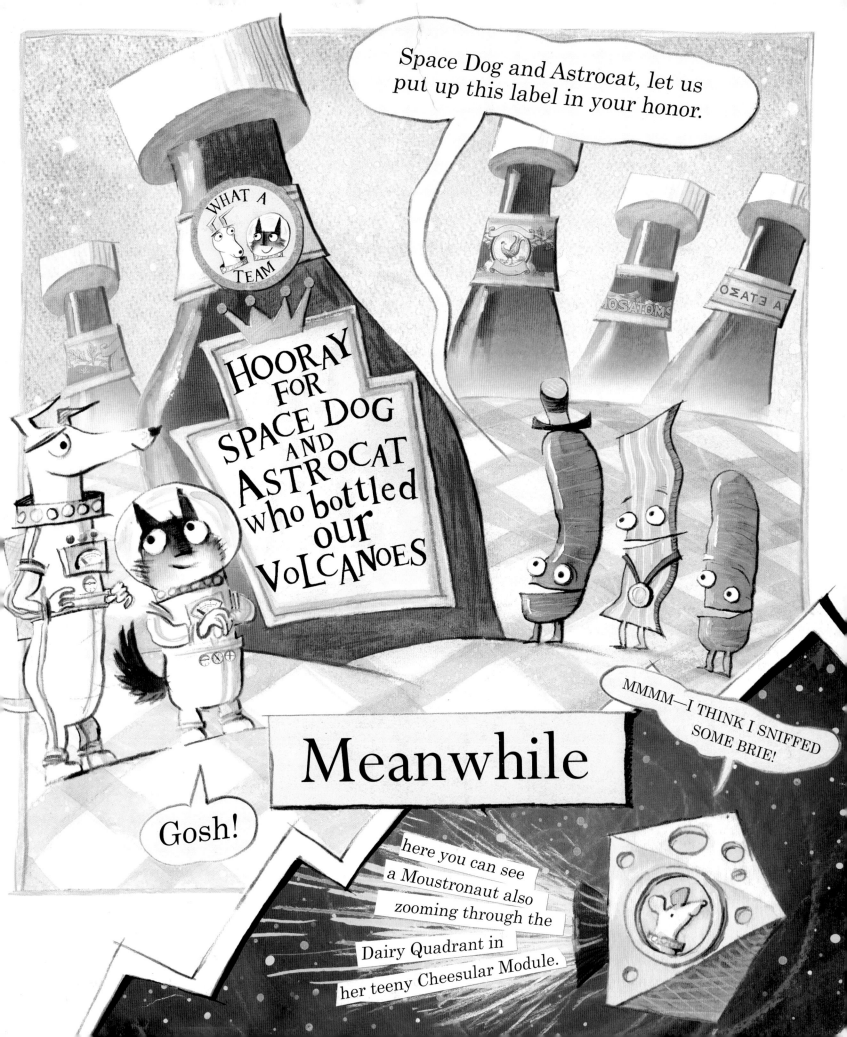

Back on the ship, Space Dog is finally setting the controls for

HOME

The UNKNOWN

when—

HOME SWEET HOME

HELP!

No la Pl

WHIFF
WHIFF

SOUVENIR OF EARTH

A distress call on the Laser Display Screen!
Coming from this distinctly cheesy planet.
They simply **have** to help.

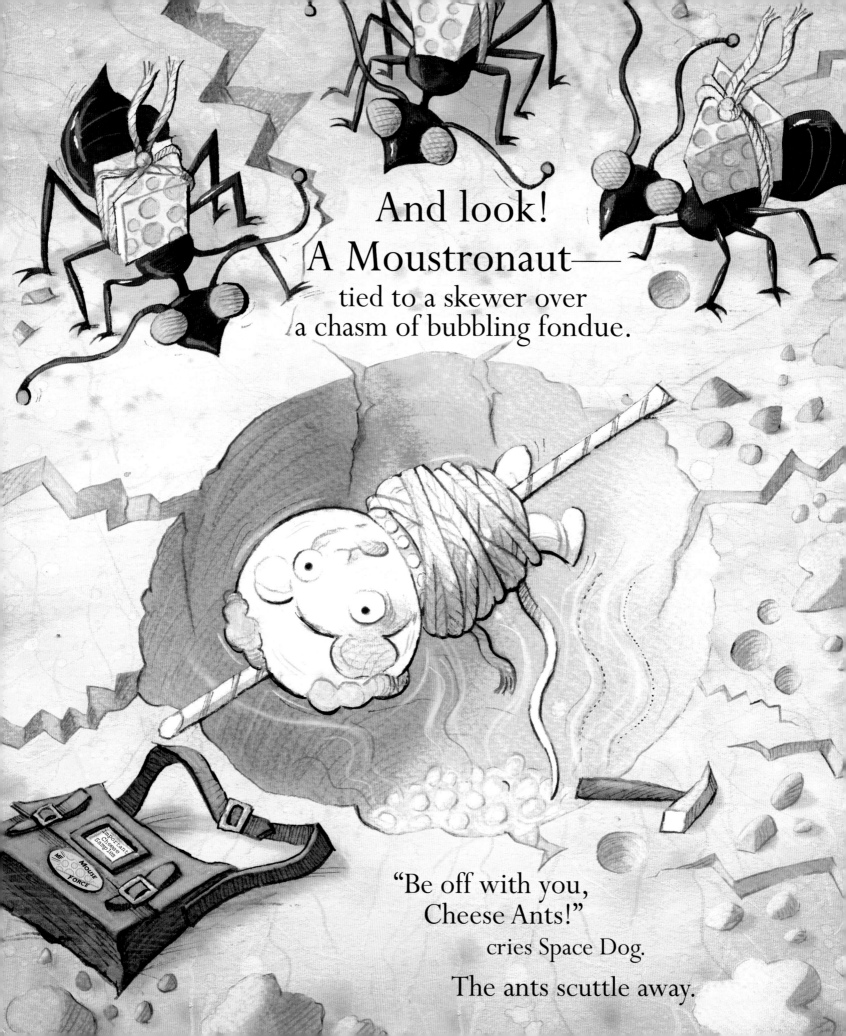

And look!
A Moustronaut—
tied to a skewer over
a chasm of bubbling fondue.

"Be off with you,
Cheese Ants!"
cries Space Dog.

The ants scuttle away.

"Grab my tail, Space Dog," says Astrocat,
balancing precariously and untangling the rope.

"BUT MOUSTRONAUTS AND ASTROCATS ARE SWORN ENEMIES!"
gasps the Moustronaut.
"But there's no time
for that now!"
Astrocat replies.

"MY SATCHEL!
MY SATCHEL!"
screams the
Moustronaut.

Astrocat grabs the satchel,
and, getting ready to run,
they turn round
to see . . .

Her mandibles are dribbling and there's a hungry look in her compound eyes.

But then the Moustronaut has an idea.

She offers the Queen the cheese samples from her satchel—

rare samples from the farthest reaches of space— and bows respectfully.

The Queen lowers her feelers.

THE CHEESE SAMPLES MUST HAVE BEEN WHAT SHE WANTED. SHE MUST BE A CHEESE COLLECTOR, TOO!

But this planet is full of holes and crumbling fast.

They dash to the ship and blast off just in time . . .

. . . as, with a lurching groan, the planet implodes.

On board Space Dog's ship, they scrape the cheesy goo off the Moustronaut, and Astrocat runs her a nice bath.

The Moustronaut has not only lost her precious cheese samples, but her Module, too.

Very Important Cheese

"Cheer up, Moustronaut," says Astrocat.
"We need a quick-thinking mouse on our team.

Someone
with nimble fingers

and amazing
powers of sniff."

"Yes," says
Space Dog.

"Someone who is brave in
the face of giant insects,

and a third player
for Dogopoly.

Now we can go Home."

BACK TO...
HOME PLANET—WHERE SPACE DOGS, ASTROCATS, AND MOUSTRONAUTS CAN BE

Cape Farewell   KITTISH ISLES   MICELAND

RADOR

ENEMIES   FOREVER

Everyone is quiet for a moment.

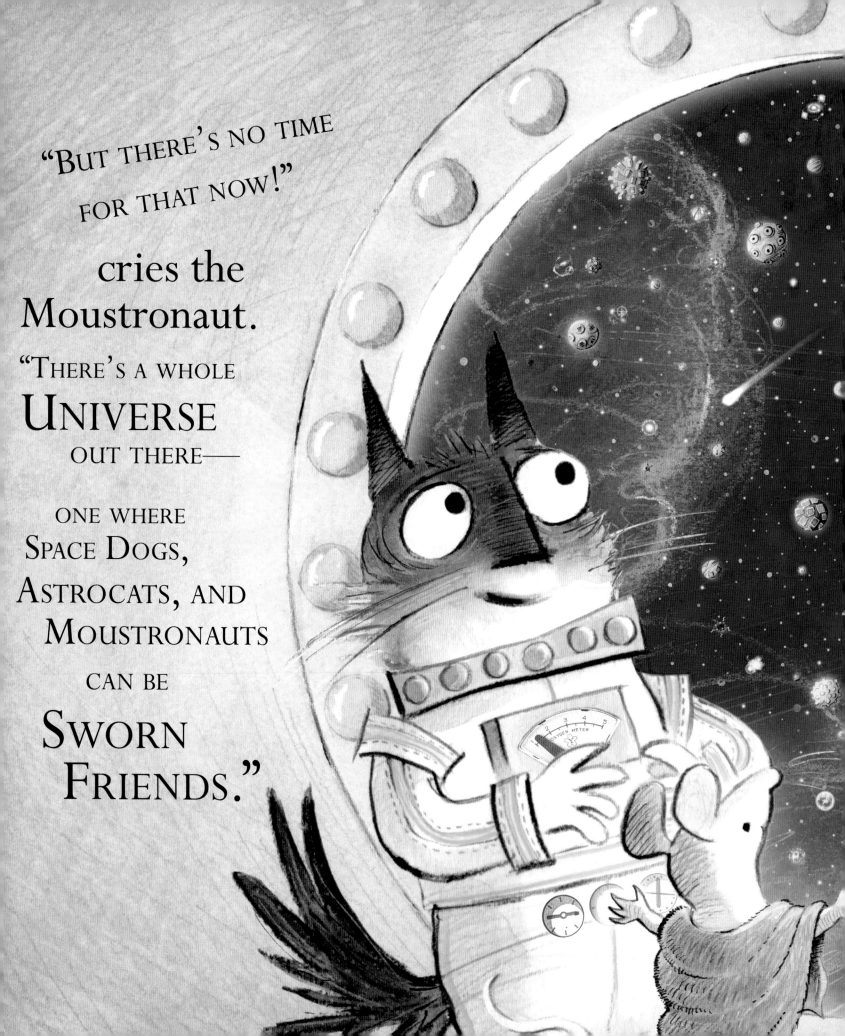

"But there's no time
for that now!"

cries the
Moustronaut.
"There's a whole
Universe
out there—

one where
Space Dogs,
Astrocats, and
Moustronauts
can be
Sworn
Friends."

HOME

Near to the
Home button
on his control panel
is another one that
Space Dog hasn't
noticed before.

The
UNKNOWN
ZONE

"Shall we?"
"Of course!"
"Why not!"

And they set
controls for
The

UNKNOWN
ZONE.

In the vast deeps of space,
a small ship is zooming.
Adventures could be
on the horizon,
or even just round
the corner.

But for now,
Space Dog, Astrocat, and
the Moustronaut are playing
Dogopoly before dinner.

Nobody is *completely* sure
of the exact rules . . .

. . . but it doesn't seem to matter.

Yoo-hoo!

Special thanks to the cosmic inspiration of Ness.

THIS IS A BORZOI BOOK PUBLISHED BY ALFRED A. KNOPF

Copyright © 2015 by Mini Grey

All rights reserved. Published in the United States by Alfred A. Knopf, an imprint of Random House Children's Books, a division of Random House LLC, a Penguin Random House Company, New York. Originally published in Great Britain by Jonathan Cape, an imprint of Random House Children's Publishers UK, a Penguin Random House Company, London, in 2015.

Knopf, Borzoi Books, and the colophon are registered trademarks of Random House LLC.

Visit us on the Web! randomhousekids.com

Educators and librarians, for a variety of teaching tools, visit us at RHTeachersLibrarians.com

Library of Congress Cataloging-in-Publication Data
Grey, Mini, author, illustrator.
Space Dog / Mini Grey. — First American edition.
pages cm.
Summary: Sworn enemies Space Dog, Astrocat, and Mousetronaut team up to save the Spooniverse.
ISBN 978-0-553-51058-4 (trade) — ISBN 978-0-553-51059-1 (lib. bdg.) —
ISBN 978-0-553-51060-7 (ebook)
[1. Dogs—Fiction. 2. Cats—Fiction. 3. Mice—Fiction. 4. Friendship—Fiction. 5. Astronauts—Fiction.
6. Heroes—Fiction. 7. Play—Fiction.] I. Title.
PZ7.G873Sp 2015 [E]—dc23 2014031623

MANUFACTURED IN CHINA

October 2015

10 9 8 7 6 5 4 3 2 1

First American Edition

For Nancy and Herbie

A GUIDE TO RARE LIFE-FORMS
OF THE OUTER SPOONIVERSE

THE SAUSAGE AND BACON
PEOPLE OF FRY UP 42

THE CRUETS OF
WEST CUTLERY

THE LEAFLETS
OF PLANET TREE

THE BROCOLLONS
OF PLANET GREENS

THE TELEVOIDS
OF ELECTRON 72

THE SCRUBBERS
OF BATHTIME 37

Name _SpaceDog_

Training Record ⭐ ⭐ ⭐